Pip

Bumble

Grubby

Aunt Tulip

Webby

Violet

Created by Keith Chapman

HarperCollins *Children's Books*

First published in Great Britain in 2005 by HarperCollins Children's Books.
HarperCollins Children's Books is a division of HarperCollins Publishers Ltd.
1 3 5 7 9 10 8 6 4 2
ISBN-13: 978-0-00-722065-6
ISBN-10: 0-00-722065-0

© Chapman Entertainment Ltd 2006
www.fifiandtheflowertots.com

Fifi and the Flowertots Story and Activity Book

Fifi and the Flowertots Story and Activity Book

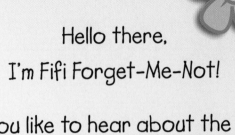

Hello there,
I'm Fifi Forget-Me-Not!

Would you like to hear about the time my
friends Bumble and Stingo had a race? Or how about
the time Stingo covered Slugsy in honey?

There are lots of stories for you to read in this
big Flowertot book! There is even a pretty picture
for you to colour in and a game to play.

My favourite story is about the time my friend
Primrose decorated Bumble's house. She was supposed
to paint it red and white but she painted it... oh Fiddly
Flowerpetals! I've forgotten what colour she used!
I suppose I'd better read it again.
Will you read along with me?

Fifi x

Contents

Contents

Bumble's Big Race

One day, Fifi was pegging out her washing.
When suddenly there was a loud...

"Whooooaaaaaaa!"

With a whirl and a twirl and a LOT of flapping, Bumble
crash-landed right in the middle of Fifi's washing!
"Oh, Bumble! Are you alright?" cried Fifi.

Stingo landed neatly on the rooftop and laughed out loud. "Lollicking Lollipops!" he teased. "Another perfect landing, eh, Bumble?"

"Bees can't fly for toffee-apples! Not like us wasps," said Stingo. "Huh! Bees are much better flyers than wasps," replied Bumble.

"Ok, I challenge you to a race!" said Stingo, "and when I win, you have to give me a jar of your honey."

Stingo promised that if Bumble won, he would buy him a big bag of buns from Poppy's stall. "Dream on, Bumble!" he said, as he flew away.

Stingo was determined to win and made a deal with Slugsy. "If you help me get fit for the race, I'll share the honey with you." said Stingo. "Oooh, yesss bosss!" agreed Slugsy.

Stingo and Slugsy started
training right away.
"Ok Slugsy, here we go!"
Stingo said.
"Let's start with skipping."

But it wasn't as easy as it
looked, especially the
trampolining!
"Sluggsssssy!!!"
yelled Stingo, as
he flew into the air.
"Owwwww!!"

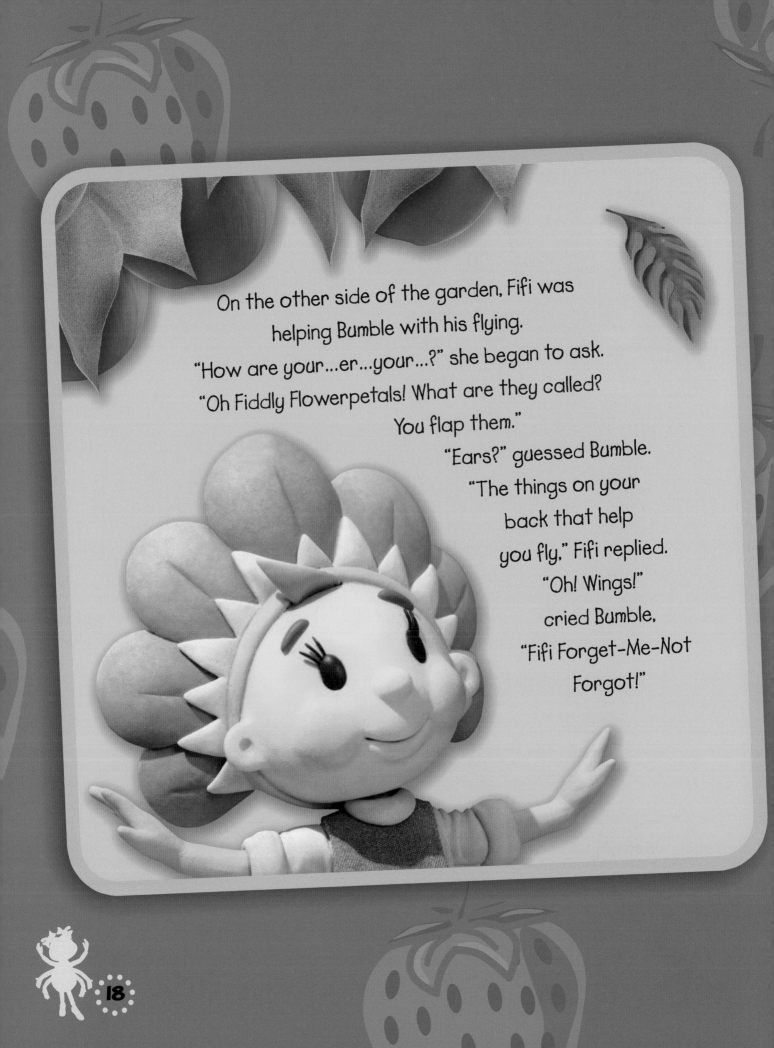

On the other side of the garden, Fifi was
helping Bumble with his flying.
"How are your...er...your...?" she began to ask.
"Oh Fiddly Flowerpetals! What are they called?
You flap them."

"Ears?" guessed Bumble.
"The things on your
back that help
you fly," Fifi replied.
"Oh! Wings!"
cried Bumble,
"Fifi Forget-Me-Not
Forgot!"

Bumble tried a landing, skidded on the grass and...
CRASH!
He ended up in a muddy heap. "I did it again! Oh, Fifi! I'm useless!" Bumble moaned. Fifi sighed and went to ask her friend Webby for advice.

Meanwhile, Stingo had been watching through his telescope. "Wasps one – Bees nil! This is going to be easy," he gloated to Slugsy. "But just in case – this is what we'll do..."

"Ommmmmmmmmm..." Webby
was relaxing in her web.
"Webby?" called Fifi.
The spider opened
her eyes.
"What's up, Fifi?"
Fifi explained about
Bumble's problem.
"Ah. Perhaps if you show
him that he's good at something
else, it'll make him feel better
about his flying,"
suggested Webby.
"That's a brilliant idea,"
smiled Fifi.

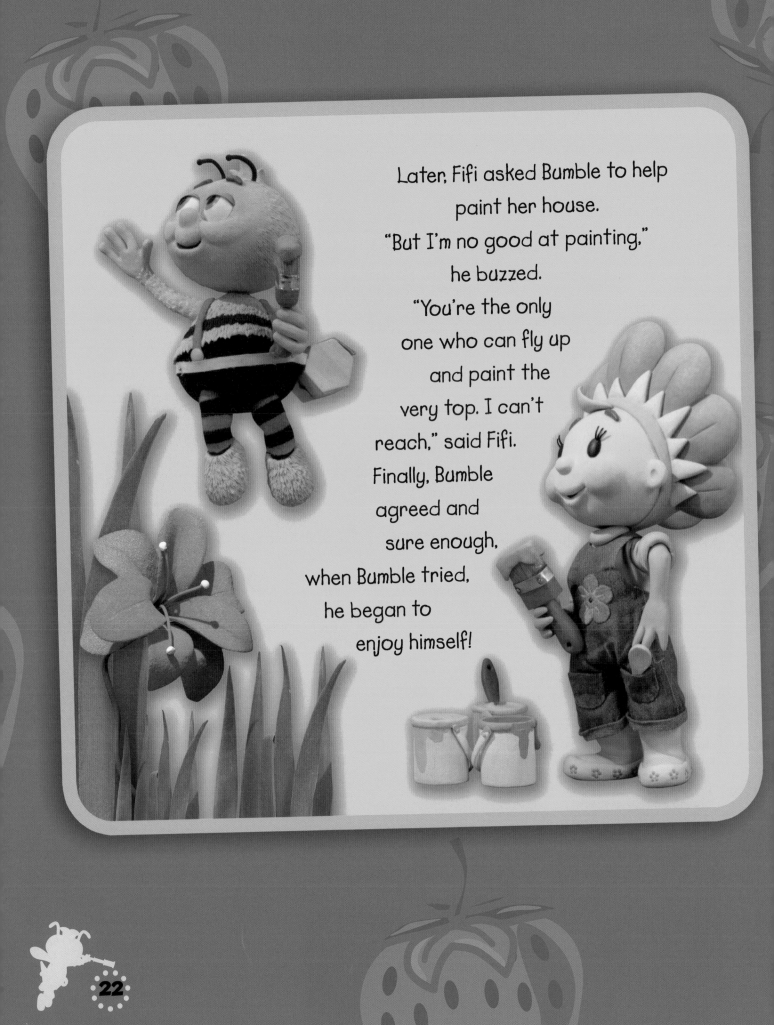

Later, Fifi asked Bumble to help paint her house.
"But I'm no good at painting," he buzzed.
"You're the only one who can fly up and paint the very top. I can't reach," said Fifi.
Finally, Bumble agreed and sure enough, when Bumble tried, he began to enjoy himself!

Even Stingo couldn't put him off! He soon gave up his teasing when a blob of paint fell off Bumble's brush and landed with a **SPLAT** right in his face!

23

Fifi and Bumble stepped back to look at the freshly painted cottage. "Brilliant job. And we only managed it because you can fly so well," said Fifi.

"Oh, yes! I think you're right, Fifi! **I AM** good at flying!" cried Bumble.

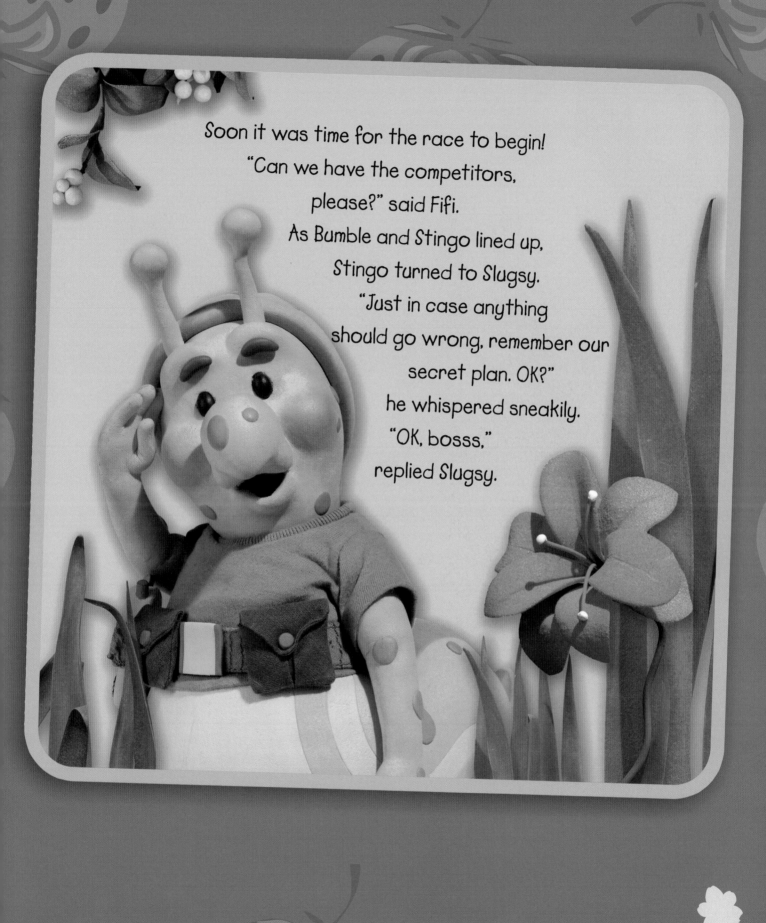

Soon it was time for the race to begin!
"Can we have the competitors,
please?" said Fifi.
As Bumble and Stingo lined up,
Stingo turned to Slugsy.
"Just in case anything
should go wrong, remember our
secret plan. OK?"
he whispered sneakily.
"OK, bosss,"
replied Slugsy.

"**GO!**" cried Stingo and sped off before Bumble.

"**Cheat!**" yelled Bumble, and flew after the naughty wasp as fast as he could.

"So long, Bumble! Hur hur," laughed Stingo.

"That is not fair!" shouted Primrose angrily.

"Stingo is going to win!" cried Violet. "We'll see," said Fifi.

"You can do it, Bumble. I know you can!"

she called.

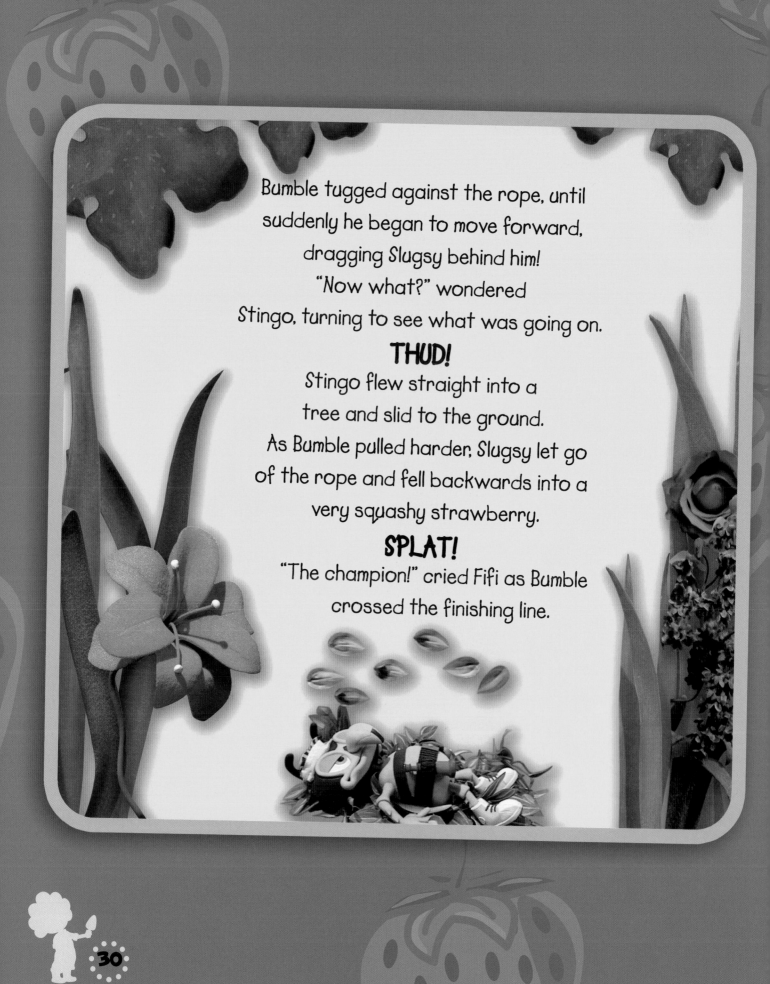

Bumble tugged against the rope, until
suddenly he began to move forward,
dragging Slugsy behind him!
"Now what?" wondered
Stingo, turning to see what was going on.

THUD!

Stingo flew straight into a
tree and slid to the ground.
As Bumble pulled harder, Slugsy let go
of the rope and fell backwards into a
very squashy strawberry.

SPLAT!

"The champion!" cried Fifi as Bumble
crossed the finishing line.

Smelly Slugsy

One sunny day, Fifi Forget-Me-Not was picking flowers to make potpourri for her friend, Poppy.

"I love potpourri!"

Fifi said to herself. Just then, Bumble buzzed into the garden. "What's potty poorly, Fifi?" he asked.

Fifi giggled. "Potpourri! It's a
mixture of herbs and flower petals
that smell nice and fresh."
"Mmm, smells lovely, Fifi," said Bumble.
"I just dropped by to tell you I heard Violet
and Primrose quarrelling just now."

"Buttercups and daisies,
not again!"

Fifi said, "I'd
better get over
there right away!"

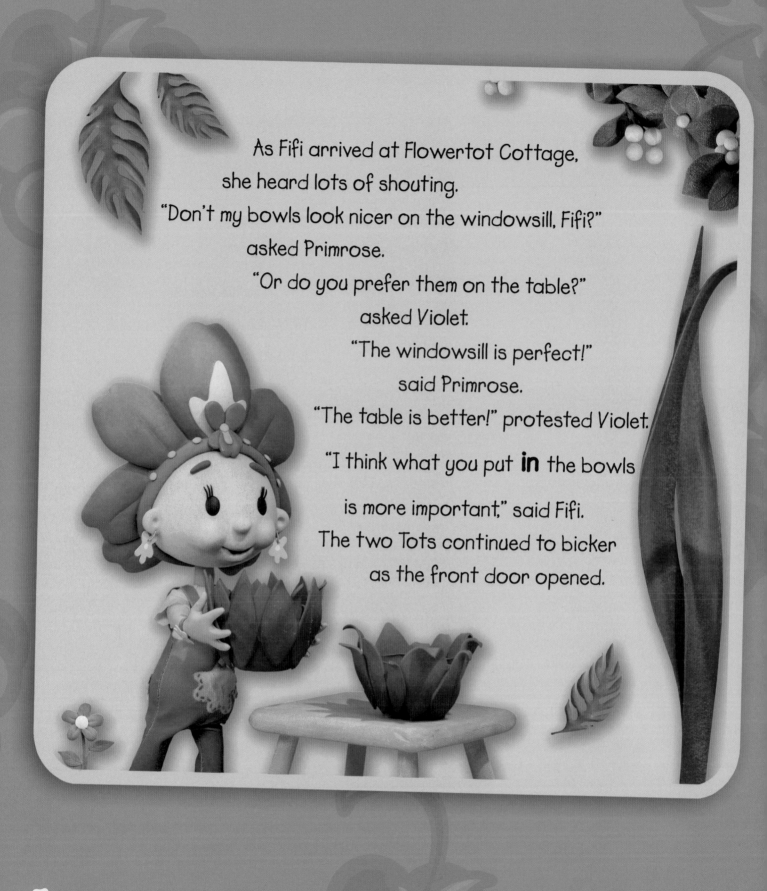

As Fifi arrived at Flowertot Cottage,
she heard lots of shouting.
"Don't my bowls look nicer on the windowsill, Fifi?"
asked Primrose.
"Or do you prefer them on the table?"
asked Violet.
"The windowsill is perfect!"
said Primrose.
"The table is better!" protested Violet.

"I think what you put **in** the bowls

is more important," said Fifi.
The two Tots continued to bicker
as the front door opened.

It was Slugsy. "Hello," he said. "Where's Stingo?" asked Fifi, suspiciously. Stingo was Slugsy's best friend and a very naughty wasp!

"I'm on my own," he said. "I want to ask Primrose sssomething very important."

"Would you like to ssshare my cauliflower tonight?"
asked Slugsy shyly.
"No! Sorry Slugsy, I can't. I'm,
er, washing my petals!"
she stammered.
"But I've taken all of the
maggots out
of the
cauliflower
for you!"
Slugsy said.

**"Maggots?
Yuck!"**

said the
Flowertots.

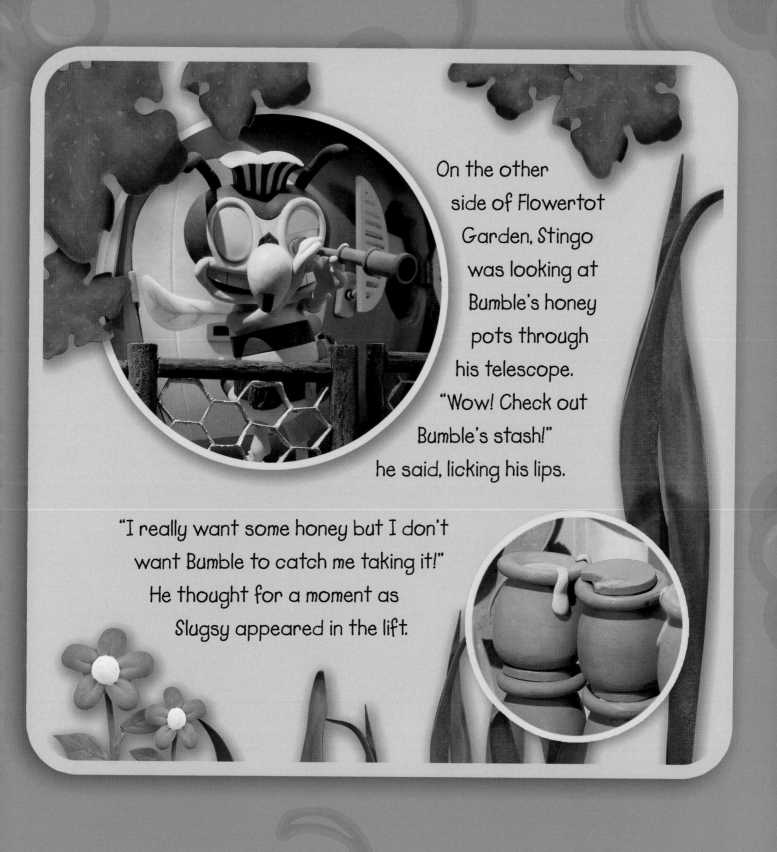

On the other side of Flowertot Garden, Stingo was looking at Bumble's honey pots through his telescope. "Wow! Check out Bumble's stash!" he said, licking his lips.

"I really want some honey but I don't want Bumble to catch me taking it!" He thought for a moment as Slugsy appeared in the lift.

"I don't think Primrose likes me, Ssstingo," said Slugsy sadly.
"Of course she doesn't like you!" exclaimed Stingo, "you're a smelly slug!"
"Then how can I make myself sssmell nicer?" Slugsy asked his pal.
Stingo smiled and threw his arm around Slugsy.
"How about a shower in something sweet and runny?" he suggested.

Soon, Stingo and Slugsy were
sneaking into Bumble's garden.
"I don't think we ssshould be
in here," Slugsy said
as Stingo flipped open
a pot of honey and poured it
all over Slugsy's back!

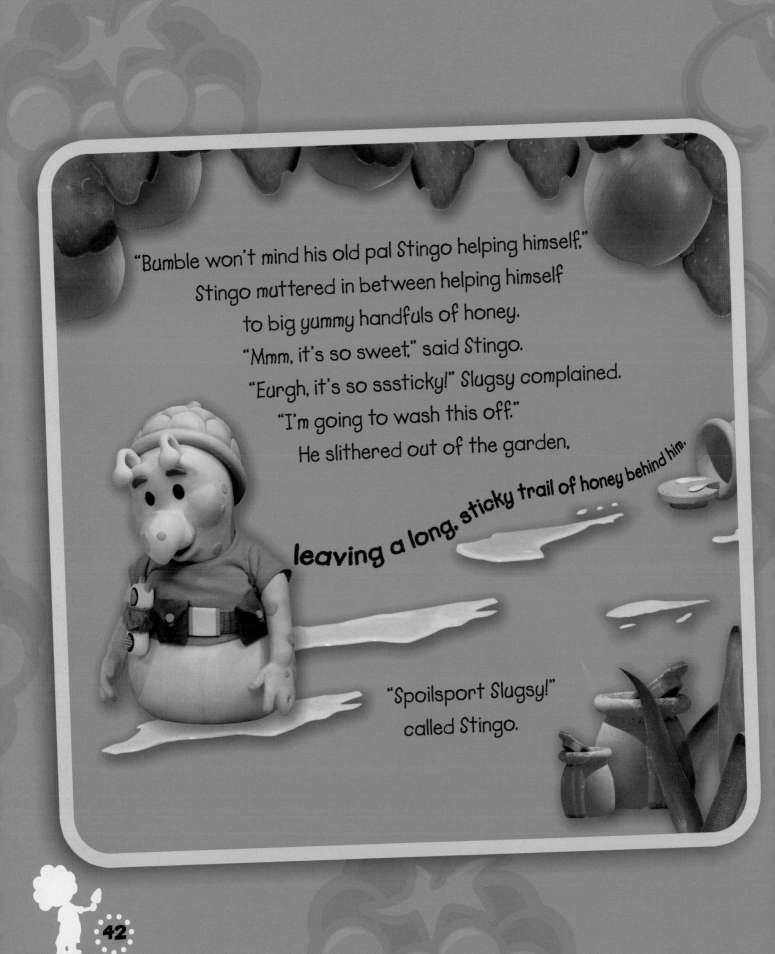

"Bumble won't mind his old pal Stingo helping himself,"
Stingo muttered in between helping himself
to big yummy handfuls of honey.
"Mmm, it's so sweet," said Stingo.
"Eurgh, it's so sssticky!" Slugsy complained.
"I'm going to wash this off."
He slithered out of the garden,

leaving a long, sticky trail of honey behind him.

"Spoilsport Slugsy!"
called Stingo.

Back in the garden, Bumble **buzzed** over Fifi's gate.

"Oh, Fifi," he said, "one of my best pots of honey has disappeared. If I help you pick some lavender for Poppy's potpourri, would you please look for my honey?"

"Oh alright then," she agreed. "I'll also need lots of..."

"Oh Fiddly Flowerpetals,
I forgot!" laughed Fifi.
"Ha-ha!" smiled Bumble

"Fifi Forget-Me-Not forgot!"
"They begin with 'r' and grow on bushes...
They have thorns and smell lovely..."
Bumble tried to guess.

"Rhubarb?

Raspberries?

Rhododendrons?"

"No, no, no..." Fifi said.

"It's roses!"

Bumble got to work while
Fifi skipped over to his
garden and searched for clues.
"Ah-ha!" she cried.
"A slimy honey slug trail.
There's only one slug in
Flowertot Garden

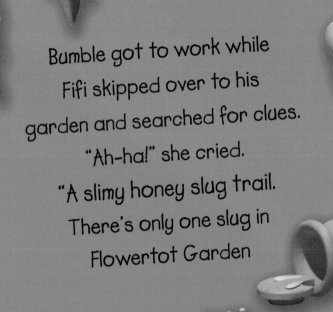

and that's Slugsy! He must
have taken Bumble's honey."

Fifi began to follow the honey trail.........

Slugsy slithered sadly into Fifi's garden.
"Er, hello Bumble," he said guiltily.
"I'm trying to find sssomething to
make me sssmell nice."
"How about lavender?" Bumble suggested.
Slugsy disappeared under Fifi's lavender bushes.
"Oooh, the lavender ssspikes are tickling me!" he giggled.
Slugsy began to laugh
louder and **louder**.
Soon all the petals were falling onto the garden.
Slugsy emerged, smiling and
covered in petals.

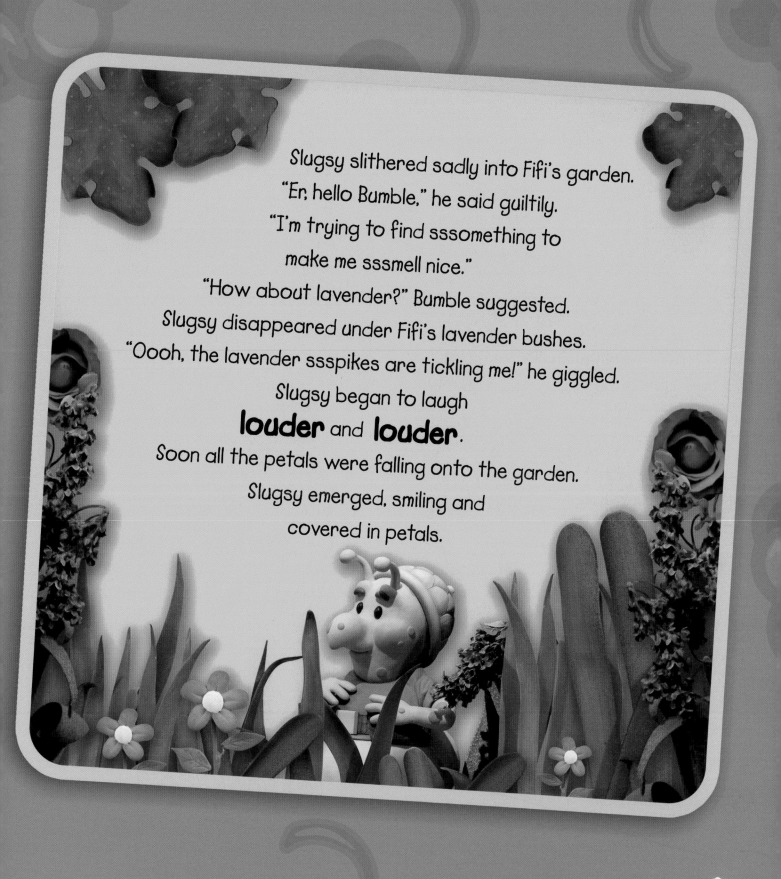

Fifi followed Slugsy's trail all the way back to her garden. "You picked those quickly, Bumble!" she said, spotting the piles of roses and lavender petals.

"It wasn't me, Fifi!" he laughed, pointing to Slugsy.

"Just the slug I'm looking for,"
Fifi said firmly.
"It wasn't me that took the honey!
It was Ssstingo!"
Slugsy blurted out.
"Stingo shouldn't take things from other people's gardens," said Fifi.
"He's a naughty, naughty wasssp!" Slugsy agreed.

"Diddly Dandelions"

exclaimed Fifi.
"Look at the time! I've got to get this potpourri to Poppy!"
"Can I help you, Fifi?"
asked Slugsy kindly.

The friends had just finished packing the potpourri
into little baskets when they heard a buzzing sound.
It was Stingo, looking for Slugsy.
"Who said you could steal a pot of Bumble's best honey?"
asked Fifi sternly.

"It was for smelly Slugsy!" Stingo protested.
"You took the honey for yourself
and then tried to blame Slugsy!"
said Fifi.
"I think you should apologise, Stingo."
Stingo looked very cross.
"Sorry, Bumble," he said.
Fifi gave Slugsy a
basket of
potpourri.
"This is to make
your house smell
nice," she said.
"I've got a much
better idea!" said Slugsy.

"I've got a present for you, Primrose," Slugsy said.

"I hope it's not cauliflower," she said, taking the basket.

"Potpourri!
Slugsy, you're a genius, this is just what I need for my new bowls." Slugsy blinked in amazement, then smiled.

"Are you sure you won't come and ssshare my cauliflower cheese?" he asked.

"Oh all right, but I'll have to wear a peg on my nose," Primrose said.

"Is it me?" asked Slugsy, ashamed.

"Oh no!" exclaimed Primrose. "I just **hate** the smell of cauliflower!"

Bumble Gets a Makeover

Early one morning in Flowertot Garden, Fifi loaded two tins of red paint, two tins of white paint and a nice, clean brush into Mo's trailer.

Fifi and Bumble had a very busy day in front of them. They were going to give Bumble's house a fresh coat of paint to brighten it up.

As Fifi arrived, Bumble was busily stacking up pots of honey and muttering to himself.

"Morning Bumble," said Fifi, "I've brought the paint!"

"Morning Fifi," said Bumble, looking confused, "whatever have you brought all that for?"

Fifi giggled. "To paint your house, remember?"

Bumble looked very embarrassed. "Oh Fifi, I forgot! I've got to label all my honey pots and collect pollen today!"

"You forgot and I remembered?" Fifi said, amazed.

"Oh dear," said Bumble, his cheeks flushing red, "and the house does need painting. It looks so tatty!"

54

"Don't worry, Bumble," Fifi smiled, "I'll paint the house while you collect your pollen!" She began unloading her paint and brushes from Mo. "I can't let you decorate the whole house all by yourself!" said Bumble, sitting amongst his empty honey pots.

"Did someone say decorating?" A familiar Flowertot voice said. It was Violet and Primrose. "We love decorating, can we help?"

"See?" said Fifi. "Go and collect your pollen Bumble. Violet, Primrose and I will paint your house."

"Thanks everyone, it does need doing. Nothing fancy, just nice white walls and a red roof." Bumble smiled as he buzzed off. Back on the ground, Fifi prised open the pots of paint and gave one to Violet and one to Primrose. "Here you go,' she said, "we'll be done in no time."

"Is this all there is?" Primrose said, peering at the red and white paint pots. "Boring!"

"This is what Bumble likes. Red for the roof and white for the walls. Nothing fancy!" Fifi said picking up a brush.

"Do you have any more paintbrushes, Fifi?" Primrose asked, eager to get started.

"Oh Fiddly Flowerpetals! I only brought one. Don't worry, I've lots more at home," Fifi hopped into Mo and set off for Forget-Me-Not Cottage.

"Hmmm, red and white is so dull," said Primrose, "I can make it look much more exciting!" She looked at the white paint pot in front of her. "I know, if I put some red in here and mix it round... Pink! The best colour there is!" Primrose began mixing the new pink paint.

"Now Violet," she called, "You can pick the daisies for the daisy chain."

"Daisy chain?" asked Violet, sounding very unsure.

"Of course. It's just what this old hive needs... the Primrose touch!" Primrose looked very pleased with herself.

Over at Forget-Me-Not Cottage, Fifi was searching for extra paintbrushes.
She looked under a stack of flowerpots and found a wooden spoon.
But no paintbrushes.
She looked under the sink and found a packet of seeds.
But no paintbrushes.
She looked by the washing machine and found some wet laundry.
But no paint brushes.

"Oh Bouncing Blueberries, I'd better put this washing out to dry!" she said to herself, forgetting all about the paintbrushes.

Violet and Primrose were hard at work. Soon Bumble had a pretty pink door and a whole rainbow of ribbons tied in bows to the outside of his house.

"Are you sure Bumble will like all these flowers, Primrose?" asked Violet as she made yet more daisy chains. "I thought he just wanted red and white..."

"Don't be silly, Violet," said
Primrose, "this is much better!"

"I don't think he's going to
recognise his own house,"
Violet said, looking doubtfully
at Primrose's design.

"Hmmm," muttered Primrose,
too busy adding the finishing
touches to hear Violet.
"Now where did Fifi get to?"

Fifi had just finished hanging out her washing when
she suddenly she remembered she was looking for something... but what?

"Fiddly Flowerpetals," she said looking all around,
"it wasn't my raincoat or my pyjamas..."

Then she spotted her paintbrushes, stood up
in a vase like flowers. "Of course, paintbrushes!
I'd better get back to Bumble's house right away!"

But when she arrived at the house,
she couldn't believe her eyes.

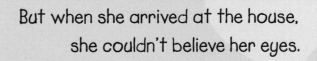

Bumble's house was covered in coloured
ribbons and flowers.
In between all the decorations,
Fifi could see a bright pink
door peeping through.

"Jumping Geraniums, Primrose,
what have you done?!" asked a shocked Fifi.

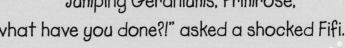

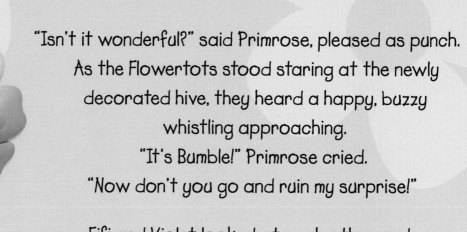

"Isn't it wonderful?" said Primrose, pleased as punch.
As the Flowertots stood staring at the newly
decorated hive, they heard a happy, buzzy
whistling approaching.
"It's Bumble!" Primrose cried.
"Now don't you go and ruin my surprise!"

Fifi and Violet looked at each other and
shook their heads, completely lost
for words.

"Hello Primrose!" Bumble
called as he spotted the
paint-splattered tot. "Is my
house finished?"

"Yes, and it's perfect!"
Primrose gushed.

As he spotted the frilly house with
the pink door his smile vanished.

"Pink?!" Bumble gasped.
"Where are my shiny white walls and my smart red roof?"

"Oh, that was boring. This is much better," Primrose said as she guided Bumble
around his new house. "I designed it all myself, you know. It was a lot of work
but just wait till you see what I've done inside."

"But what happened to my simple home?"
Bumble was beginning to lose his temper.
"I want my house back!"

"But this is better," explained Primrose calmly, "I've even decorated that old honey tap of yours. See, you just turn it on like this," Primrose delved under a big pile of ribbons and turned Bumble's honey tap but some of the ribbons got stuck...

"Then you turn it off, like this," Primrose began wrestling with the tap but it just wouldn't budge. Soon honey began to glug everywhere.

"My honey!" Bumble wailed. "Fifi, do something!"

Fifi quickly grabbed a paper garland and stuffed it up the tap, stopping the runny honey.

Primrose looked around at the piles of honey covered ribbons and garlands. "I was only trying to help," she sniffed.

"I'm sure we can sort this out," Fifi said, "why don't we just redecorate the way Bumble likes it?"

"Red roof?" Violet said. Bumble nodded.

"White walls?" Fifi suggested. Bumble nodded.

"And no ribbons, flowers or pink paint!" He added.

"Alright," agreed Primrose.

Soon, Bumble's little house was
back just the way he liked it.
Primrose sat sadly with a big pile
of ribbons and daisy chains.
"Sorry I ruined everything Bumble,"
she said,
"I suppose I'd better throw these away."
Fifi quickly whispered something to
Bumble who nodded happily.

"Good idea, Fifi! We can use the ribbon to tie around the lids of
the honey pots! A different colour for each different flavour.
Pink for rose honey, green for apple honey..."

"And orange for orange honey!" Primrose said happily, tying a big
bow around the honey pot, "Oh, they look so pretty!"

"Now everyone is happy!" Fifi smiled as she
started off towards Mo.

"Oh, Fifi wait!" Primrose called,
"Fifi, I've had some great
decorating ideas for Forget-Me-Not
Cottage. Shall I come over and show
you them later?"

Bumble and Violet stifled a giggle.

"I think we've all done quite enough decorating
for one day, don't you?" Fifi laughed.

Goodbye from Fifi and Bumble!

Stingo

Fifi

Primrose

Poppy

Slugsy

Mo